Friday the Thirteenth

by

David Webb

D1464546

Illustrated by Derry Dillon

38067200024298

First published
January 08 in Great Britain by

SLOUGH LIBRARY & INFORMATION	
38067200024298	
CF	21-Feb-08
PETERS	

© **David Webb 2008**

The moral right of the author has been asserted in accordance with the
Copyright, Designs and Patents Act 1988

ISBN-10 1-905637-37-3
ISBN-13 978-1-905637-37-9

Educational Printing Services Limited
Albion Mill, Water Street, Great Harwood, Blackburn BB6 7QR
Telephone: (01254) 882080   Fax: (01254) 882010
E-mail: enquiries@eprint.co.uk   Website: www.eprint.co.uk

Contents

Chapter 1
Friday the Thirteenth

'No! No! No!' yelled Callum, as he thrashed his arms and kicked out at the great, dark shape. 'Get off me, you brute! Someone help! Save me!'

The bear charged again, its eyes wide, saliva dripping from its huge yellow-white teeth.

'Please help me! Won't someone help me?'

'Callum!' snapped his mum, crossly. 'Will you come out from underneath that quilt! You've been having one of your nightmares again!'

Callum crawled slowly up the bed and pushed his head out from beneath the quilt. His face was red and his hair stuck up like a lavatory brush.

'It . . .it . . . was a bear,' he stammered. 'I was fighting with a great, angry, brown bear.'

'Look at the state of that bed,' complained Mum. 'It looks like a shipwreck! Anyway, you'll have to get a move on or else you'll be late for school. It's twenty minutes to nine.'

'Twenty to nine!' repeated Callum, sitting bolt upright in bed. 'How come it's twenty to nine?'

'The alarm clock didn't go off again,' replied Mum. 'It was only your father's snoring that woke me up!'

'I'm going to get into real trouble,' groaned Callum, leaping out of bed. 'This will be my third time late this week.'

'Well, it *is* Friday the thirteenth,' said Mum. 'Not a lucky day. You'll have to take care.'

'*Friday the thirteenth,*' mocked Callum, in a sing-song voice. 'What difference does that make? I don't believe in all those silly, old fashioned superstitions, you know. *Friday the thirteenth,* indeed!'

Two minutes later, Callum was hammering on the bathroom door. His sister Selina had locked herself inside and Callum knew exactly what that meant. Selina could take up to an hour to get herself ready.

'Selina! Will you open the door!' demanded Callum. 'I'm going to be late for school!'

There was a gasp and a wail from inside the locked bathroom. 'Oh, no!' moaned Selina. 'I've got a spot on my chin!'

'You've got spots all over your face!' shouted Callum, in anger. 'One more isn't going to make any difference! Now will you open the door!'

'I knew it was going to be a bad day,' whimpered Selina. 'It's Friday the thirteenth!'

Breakfast was very rushed. Callum didn't bother to sit down. He took a slurp of tea and shoved a piece of toast in his mouth as he struggled to fasten his school tie. A blob of strawberry jam slid off his toast and landed on the front of his white school shirt.

'I don't believe it!' sighed Callum. He tried to rub it off with his finger but the sticky mess spread wider. 'This is a disaster!'

'Here, let me help you,' said his mum, arriving with a damp cloth. 'I don't think anyone will notice.'

Selina appeared at the kitchen door, a blob of white cream smeared on her chin.

'Had a little accident, have you?' she said, grinning at the spreading red stain. 'That looks a right mess.'

'Reminds me of one of your spots,' said Callum, cruelly. 'Except it's not as big and it's not as red.'

Selina burst into tears and ran back upstairs.

'There was no need for that!' snapped Callum's mum. 'I don't know why you two have to be so horrible to each other.'

Callum frowned and shoved the rest of the toast into his mouth.

❁ ❁ ❁

A couple of minutes later Callum was ready to leave. If he was lucky, he might just catch the last school bus.

'It's cold out there,' fussed Mum, opening the front door. 'Fasten up your coat and wrap that nice scarf around your neck.'

Callum hated his scarf. His grandma had knitted it for his birthday and it was awful. Reluctantly, he wound it three times around his neck and then stepped out into the cold.

'And do take care,' shouted Mum, as he made his way down the front path. 'Remember – it's Friday the thirteenth!'

Chapter 2
Callum in the Cold

It was a bitterly cold morning. A
shimmering white frost covered the
rooftops, the bare trees and the garden
fences. A few fluttering flakes drifted down
slowly from the pale, grey sky. Callum could
see his breath in the freezing air as he
made his way along the pavement. He needed
to hurry if he was going to catch the school
bus but it was impossible. He slipped and slid
and wobbled along as best he could. He was

actually quite glad he was wearing Grandma's stripy scarf – even if it did trail down almost to the ground!

Callum rounded the corner at the bottom of the street just in time to see the school bus pull away from the stop. Three of his friends were on the back seat and they waved and pulled faces at him as he stood and stared in frustration.

He had never really noticed the number before but there it was, as clear as clear could be, a big black number **13** on the back of the bus. The number seemed to leap out at him as the bus disappeared into the distance.

'I don't believe it!' muttered Callum, and he thrust his hands deep into his pockets. 'How unlucky is that!'

A little bit further along the road Callum met Mr Hobson, his next door neighbour, who was taking his dog Jasper for an early morning walk. Callum was usually quite fond of dogs but Jasper was a nasty, bad-tempered creature that always seemed to be slobbering and snarling. It often kept him awake at night with its constant barking.

'Good morning, Mr Hobson,' said Callum politely, keeping one eye on the growling dog. 'It's a bit chilly, isn't it?'

'Freezing,' replied Mr Hobson. 'Jasper doesn't like the cold. It makes him irritable.'

The dog was glaring at Callum. It bared its yellow teeth and growled again, threateningly, like a rumbling volcano about to erupt.

'Yes, he does look a bit irritable,' agreed Callum, nodding his head. 'I know exactly how he feels! Well, I must be going; I'm already late for school.'

He was just about to move when the dog attacked. It leapt up at him snarling like a demon.

'No, Jasper!' shouted Mr Hobson, pulling

in vain at the dog's lead. 'Bad dog! Leave him alone!'

Jasper's huge paws thumped against Callum's chest sending him reeling backwards into a garden hedge. At the same time, the dog sank its teeth into Callum's stripy scarf and shook it like a cornered rat. The scarf tightened around Callum's neck and he gasped and spluttered as the dog tugged at it.

'Get off it!' yelled Mr Hobson in despair. 'Bad dog! Leave it alone!'

Callum managed to yank the scarf free just as Mr Hobson pulled the dog away. Jasper's eyes were wild and he had bits of coloured wool hanging from his drooling jaws.

'Awfully sorry,' said an embarrassed Mr Hobson, 'he's in a bad mood this morning because it's so cold. Still, no harm done, eh?'

And with that, Mr Hobson walked off dragging the drooling dog behind him.

'No harm done!' muttered Callum, pulling himself out of the hedge. 'I'm scratched, filthy dirty and my favourite scarf's ripped to shreds! No harm done, indeed! Surely nothing else can go wrong today!'

Chapter 3

Baz and Spud

Callum was feeling thoroughly miserable as he hurried along the road towards Rubble Street School. Mrs Senior, Callum's class teacher, didn't like her children being late and Friday was her duty day. He glanced down at his Homer Simpson watch. It was a couple of minutes to nine. Doh! He might just make it. He might just be able to sneak onto the back of the line as his class waited its turn to file into school.

Callum tried to break into a run but it was difficult. The pavement was slippery with the morning frost and he tottered and slid down the street. A window cleaner was half way up his ladder, which reached across the pavement outside the newsagent's shop.

'Can't walk underneath a ladder,' mumbled Callum, stepping carefully around it, into the road. 'It's bad luck – and it's Friday the thirteenth!' And then he remembered that he didn't believe in such silly superstitions and he muttered, 'What nonsense!'

He rounded the corner into Rubble Street. Good! He was about a minute away from school and the morning bell was only just ringing. He could hear it in the chill, crisp air. Callum quickened his pace again – only to be stopped in his tracks by two scruffy teenagers who stepped from the shelter of a shop doorway and blocked the pavement in front of him.

'Excuse me,' said Callum politely and he tried to step around them.

One of the youths moved sideways so

that he couldn't get past. 'In a hurry, are we?' The youth was wearing a black, leather jacket. He had a huge, gold, heart-shaped medallion around his neck and he was chewing gum.

'Yes, I am, actually,' replied Callum. He wasn't scared, he was just annoyed at being held up. 'I'm late for school.'

'Late for school,' mocked the other youth, in a sing-song voice. He was wearing a dark green top with the hood pulled up over his head. Callum could only just see his face, which was spotty like his sister's.

'Can I get past, please?' said Callum, firmly.

'Well, let me see, now?' said the first youth. 'What do you think, Spud? Shall we let him past?'

Callum could see why he was called
Spud. His spotty face looked exactly like a
potato.

'Ooh, I don't know about that,' said
Spud, rubbing his lumpy chin. 'What d'you
think, Baz? I'll tell you what – you can get
past if you give us your dinner money.'

'I haven't got any dinner money,' said Callum. 'I bring sandwiches.' And then he groaned in frustration as he realised he'd left his sandwiches at home.

'He brings sandwiches, Spud. That's not much good to us, is it?' said Baz.

'No good at all,' agreed Spud, pulling a sour face. 'I don't like sandwiches. I've never liked sandwiches!'

Callum had just about had enough. He was usually calm but something snapped inside him. He swung out his foot and caught Spud just below the knee. Spud sank to the floor in pain as an astonished Baz looked on. Callum took his chance. He dashed between the two youths and escaped before they had realised what had happened.

Callum glanced back briefly, just as he was about to enter the school gates. He smiled to himself in satisfaction. He had never done anything like that before. Still, it served them right!

Chapter 4
The Supply Teacher

The children were already in their lines when Callum entered the school playground. To his surprise, there was no sign of Mrs Senior. Instead, a stern looking man dressed in a brown suit stood before the assembled children, scowling at each line in turn. He was tall and thin and very bony. His pale ginger hair was swept back and combed carefully over the top of his head.

'Stand still, lad!' he snapped at one of the younger boys. 'Surely you have been taught to stand still in your lines!'

Callum crept across the playground, hoping that this fierce new teacher would not notice him. He was about to join the back of his line when the teacher glared in his direction.

'Well boy?' he demanded. 'What have you got to say for yourself?'

'Good morning Mr . . . er . . . .'

'Wiggins,' snapped the teacher, 'Mr Wiggins.' A few of the younger children giggled – until he glared at them. 'And I'm still waiting for an explanation, boy? What have you got to say for yourself?'

'Sorry I'm late, Mr Wiggle,' said Callum,

quietly. He was totally embarrassed. "I'm afraid I overslept.'

Mr Wiggins' bony face seemed to darken to a shade of pale purple. 'The name is Wiggins!' he snapped. 'And what do you mean you overslept? What would happen if everyone overslept, boy? What would happen if I overslept? We'd have an empty school, wouldn't we boy?'

'Yes, Sir,' agreed Callum, thinking it was most unlikely.

'Well, I hope you're wide awake now boy because I am taking your class today. Mrs Senior isn't very well so you will have the pleasure of my company.'

'Thank you, Sir,' said Callum, joining his line – and then under his breath he muttered, 'Friday the thirteenth!'

The morning got no better for Callum. There was a note on the teacher's desk asking Mr Wiggins to collect in the maths homework and Callum realised in horror that he had left his on the kitchen table. He could see it now. It was right next to his sandwich box, which he had also forgotten! There was nothing for it – he would have to admit it.

Callum's hand crept slowly into the air as the maths books were passed forward to the front of the class.

Mr Wiggins' eyes narrowed. He guessed there was a problem.

'P – pl – please, Sir,' began Callum, nervously, 'I've left my maths book at home.'

'Bad luck,' whispered Lisa Brooks, who sat behind Callum.

'Wouldn't like to be in your shoes!' added Michael Jones, who sat to one side.

There was a moment's pause and then, very slowly, the angry teacher pointed a long, bony finger towards Callum as the victim squirmed in his seat.

'This boy has not bothered to do his maths homework, children! What do you think of that?'

No one answered at first but then William Snelling shook his head and said, 'It's awful, Sir. It's happened before, you know.'

William Snelling was a nasty little sneak who had a permanently snotty nose. Callum glared at him.

'This boy would rather watch television or play computer games than do his maths homework! What do you think of that?'

William Snelling tutted, sniffed loudly and shook his head again.

'I've done the work,' said Callum, indignantly. 'I've just not brought it in. I was late for school, you see.'

'I know you were late for school!' stormed Mr Wiggins. His face was like a boiled beetroot by now. 'We all know you were late for school, boy!'

'Sorry, Sir,' sighed Callum, sinking lower in his chair. 'It's Friday the thirteenth!'

Chapter 5
The New Girl

The new girl arrived just before assembly. The classroom door opened and Mrs Morris, the Headteacher, entered with a huge smile on her face. She was followed closely by a rather plump lady who had a shock of vivid red hair. The new girl, looking very nervous, was holding tightly onto her mother's hand.

'Now, pay attention,' began Mrs Morris.

'This is Daisy and she is joining our school today. I've told her what lovely children you are and I want you all to make her feel very welcome.'

Callum stared at the new girl. She looked exactly like her mother – a shock of red hair and a face full of freckles.

'Come on in, Daisy and meet your new classmates,' continued Mrs Morris, ignoring a few giggles and sniggers from the back of the class. 'Lovely children, aren't they Mr Wiggins?'

'Er . . . yes . . . quite . . . lovely,' agreed Mr Wiggins through gritted teeth.

'Now, I don't know if Mrs Senior had sorted out a place for Daisy,' said Mrs Morris, glancing around the room. 'Perhaps I could leave that to you, Mr Wiggins?'

Callum's blood ran cold. He glanced at the empty seat next to him – the only spare seat in the class – and he felt a sinking feeling in his stomach. Callum knew what was coming next.

'Oh, I think I've got just the place for Daisy,' said Mr Wiggins, with a sly grin. 'You leave her with me, Mrs Morris, I know just the person to look after her.'

Daisy let go of her mother's hand reluctantly and gave her a goodbye kiss. It was only when she turned back to look at the sea of faces before her that she spotted the spare seat next to Callum and her freckled face broke into a satisfied smile.

Five minutes later Daisy was in her new place next to Callum, looking very pleased with herself.

'This is very nice, isn't it Callum?' she whispered, giving him her best grin. 'I think I'm going to like it here after all.'

William Snelling sniffed, sniggered and giggled with delight.

Callum grimaced and held his head in his hands as Mr Wiggins wrote the dreaded date across the top of the board.

Break time was a nightmare.

'You make sure you look after Daisy,' instructed Mr Wiggins, as the children made their way out of class. 'Don't you leave her on her own on her first day, will you Callum?'

Some hope. Daisy was sticking to him like glue. Whenever he moved, Daisy moved too.

'Wouldn't you like to go and play with some of the girls?' suggested Callum, as the children spilled into the playground. 'I'm sure you'll get on well with them.'

A group of his friends pointed and laughed and blew kisses at them.

'No thanks,' said Daisy, doing her best to smile sweetly. 'I'd much rather stay with you, Callum. We're going to get on really well, aren't we Callum?'

'Oh, fantastic!' replied Callum, sarcastically. 'I'm so glad you're sitting next to me!' And he set off at a brisk pace across the school playground, Daisy doing her best to keep up with him.

Chapter 6
Visitors at the Gate

Within minutes, Mr Wiggins was out in the school yard on playground duty. It was still freezing cold and the teacher was clutching tight hold of a mug of hot coffee.

'No escape,' muttered Callum, thrusting his hands deep into his trouser pockets.

William Snelling sauntered past and sniggered again.

'I think we should play a game,' said Daisy, moving a little closer to Callum. 'It's far too cold just to stand around. What would you like to play, Callum?'

Callum took a step back and said, 'I'd like to play football with my mates.'

It was as if Daisy had not heard him. She shuffled closer again, put her hand on his arm and said, 'I've got a skipping rope in my bag, Callum. Shall I go back inside and get it? I could teach you how to skip.'

'Good idea,' agreed Callum, seeing a glimmer of hope. 'You go back inside and get your rope and I'll wait right here for you.'

Daisy looked a little surprised but she gave a big smile and trotted off happily towards the school entrance.

❋ ❋ ❋

Callum took his chance. He waited for her to disappear through the door and then he raced across to the opposite side of the school yard and stood beside the bins. There was a good chance the dreadful Daisy wouldn't see him there.

He was just feeling pleased with himself when he noticed something strange. Mr Wiggins was striding purposefully towards the school gate and there, leaning against the gateposts were Baz and Spud, the two thugs who had threatened Callum earlier that morning.

'He's going to chase them away,' said Callum to himself, and he nodded in satisfaction. Maybe Mr Wiggins wasn't that bad after all.

But Mr Wiggins didn't chase them away.
To Callum's surprise, he stood at the gate
chatting to them, staring around suspiciously
every so often.

'That's strange,' muttered Callum,
scratching his head. 'How does Mr Wiggins
know those two thugs? That's very strange
indeed.'

Callum watched as the teacher shook hands with Baz and patted Spud on the back. He gave them a friendly wave before moving back into the main part of the school yard.

❄ ❄ ❄

Suddenly, a shrill voice brought Callum back to reality.

'There you are!' trilled Daisy. She was standing in front of him grinning like a cat that had got the cream. 'I couldn't find you for a moment but that nice boy pointed you out.'

Callum glared across at William Snelling, who was doubled up with laughter.

'I've got my rope,' continued Daisy, holding it up in front of Callum's face. 'Come along, Callum, I'll teach you how to skip!'

Chapter 7
The Computer Unit

Back in class, Callum was talking to a couple of the other children. There was something bothering him about Mr Wiggins and he had decided to confide in his friends. Daisy was hovering at his shoulder, all the time trying to edge closer.

'There's something strange about him,' said Callum. 'Why was he talking to those two thugs at the school gate?'

'Perhaps he knew them,' suggested Harry Stubbs. 'He might have taught them sometime in the past.'

'But why would they turn up here today?' argued Callum. 'It doesn't make sense.'

'I think Mr Wiggins seems very nice,' interrupted Daisy. 'After all, he sat me next to you, didn't he, Callum?'

'Exactly my point,' snapped Callum. 'He's weird! I'm telling you, there's something very strange about that man!'

Callum stared at his friends, who had suddenly fallen silent, and he knew instantly that Mr Wiggins had entered the room and was standing behind him.

'Dear, oh dear, oh dear,' said the

teacher, stepping forward. His arms were folded across his chest and his frowning face was darkening by the second. 'I do hope you're not talking about anyone I might know, Callum?'

'No, Sir . . . ' lied Callum. 'It . . . it was just a character from a television programme I've been watching.'

'I see,' scowled the teacher. 'Perhaps a little less T.V. and a little more homework would be a good idea! Now, back to your places, everyone!'

That same afternoon, the children were allowed to use the laptop computers. It was Callum's job, together with his friend Harry, to fetch the computer storage unit from the stockroom and to share out the laptops one between two. Much to his dismay, Mr

Wiggins told Callum to share with Daisy.

'But I always work with Harry,'
protested Callum. 'Harry and I always share
a computer.'

'Well you're not today, are you lad?'
snapped Mr Wiggins, flattening his wispy
hair with the palm of his hand. 'Now get on
with your work lad!'

Callum scowled and sat back down next
to Daisy – and there she was, smiling back at
him, all teeth and freckles.

At the end of the afternoon, Callum and
Harry collected in the laptops and stacked
them away carefully on the storage unit.
They were just about to wheel the unit back
to the stockroom when Mr Wiggins stopped
them.

'I didn't ask you to move the unit,' he growled, 'just leave it where it is, please.'

'But Mrs Senior always asks us to lock the computer unit away,' protested Callum. 'It's part of our job.'

'I said *leave it*!' snapped the teacher. 'Off you go home!'

Callum and Harry exchanged suspicious glances and then backed away from the storage unit. There was nothing they could do; they would have to obey the teacher – but Callum felt very uneasy.

Daisy was waiting for Callum outside the classroom door.

'I thought we could walk home together, Callum. That would be nice, wouldn't it?'

'Must rush,' said Harry, doing his best to stifle a snigger, and then he dashed off down the corridor.

'That would be *wonderful*!' sighed Callum, sarcastically and then under his breath he muttered: *'Friday the thirteenth!'*

Chapter 8
Back to School

Callum's mood was turning from bad to worse. He set off for home with his hands in his pockets and his head down, walking as quickly as he could so that Daisy struggled to keep up. She was chattering endlessly. She hardly took a breath between sentences.

'Do you have any pets, Callum? I've got a tabby cat called Mister Tickle! He's ever so funny. D'you know what he does? He runs up the curtains and hangs there like a bat. What d'you think of that, Callum?'

'I hate cats,' muttered Callum. 'Flea-ridden creatures, if you ask me.'

And then he stopped suddenly and clasped a hand to his forehead. 'Oh, no!' he moaned. 'I don't believe it!'

Daisy was so surprised that she walked into the back of him.

'Whatever's the matter, Callum? Aren't you feeling well?'

'I've forgotten my maths homework,' sighed Callum. 'I've left it in my tray at school. Wiggle will go mad at me tomorrow morning! I'll have to go back for it.'

'Don't worry,' said Daisy, reassuringly. 'I'm in no hurry to get home; I'll go back with you.'

Five minutes later, Callum and Daisy were back at the school gates. Daisy was still twittering on about her cat. Callum was just about to tell her to shut up when he stopped and stared across the yard towards the classroom window.

'What's the matter?' asked Daisy, sensing that there was something wrong.

Callum raised one hand very slowly and pointed.

'It's them,' he said, and he moved to one side so that he was peering around the gatepost. 'They're in the classroom!'

'Who's in the classroom?' asked Daisy, looking puzzled.

'Those two thugs who stopped me on the way to school this morning,' replied Callum. 'The ugly one is called Spud and I think his friend is called Baz.'

'What are they doing in our classroom?' asked Daisy, edging closer to Callum. Secretly, she was pleased that Callum had started to talk to her.

'That's what I'd like to know,' replied Callum, scratching his head. 'In fact, I'm going to find out. You stay here, Daisy. If I'm not back in ten minutes go straight to the Headteacher's room and tell Mrs Morris what you've seen.'

'All right, Callum,' said Daisy, nodding her head. 'Take care, won't you?'

Callum scowled at her, took a deep breath and walked confidently across the school yard towards the main entrance.

❄ ❄ ❄

Inside, the school was eerily quiet. Callum crept along the corridor towards the classroom. He was breathing heavily and, despite the bitterly cold day, a light sweat had broken on his brow. He turned right at the end of the corridor and then pulled up with a start – for there, standing right in front of him blocking his way, was Mr Wiggins. His arms were folded and the familiar frown seemed even deeper.

'Dear, oh dear, oh dear,' he began, taking a step forward. 'Late arriving this morning and now late going home! It's not your lucky day, is it lad? What are you doing back in school?'

Callum decided to tell the truth. 'I'm sorry, Mr Wiggins, but I forgot my homework and then I saw two older boys in the classroom. I think they might be stealing our computers.'

Mr Wiggins narrowed his eyes and scratched his chin. 'Well that's very serious, Callum. Come on, we'd better take a look! You lead the way!'

Suddenly, Callum felt more relaxed. Perhaps Mr Wiggins was not so bad after all. He pushed past the teacher and walked confidently up to the classroom door. Callum pushed open the door and stepped inside. Sure enough, they were there! Baz and Spud froze immediately. They had been caught red handed! Spud was clutching hold of a laptop and Baz was holding open a sack.

'I knew it!' gasped Callum in satisfaction. 'They're stealing our computers!'

There was a sudden slam behind him and Callum spun around to see Mr Wiggins standing with his back against the classroom door. He had a look of pure evil on his purple face.

Chapter 9
Daisy to the Rescue

'What shall we do with him?' asked Baz.
He had gripped Callum by the collar and
forced an arm behind his back.

'Shove him in the stockroom!' ordered
Mr Wiggins. 'I've got the key. With a bit of
luck, no one will find him until tomorrow
morning.'

'You won't get away with this!' protested

Callum, as he was forced across the classroom towards the stockroom door. 'Mrs Morris knows I'm here! She'll be along in a moment!'

'Shut up!' snapped Mr Wiggins. 'You've been trouble since I set eyes on you first thing this morning. It will do you good to be locked up for the night!'

Baz gave one final push and Callum lurched forward into the stockroom, stumbling into a pile of books. The door slammed shut and Callum heard a click as the key turned in the lock. He was trapped. There was no way out.

❁ ❁ ❁

Outside, Daisy was growing anxious. Callum had said to wait for ten minutes and then go and find Mrs Morris. The ten minutes were almost up and there was no sign of Callum. She was worried about her mother, too. Daisy had promised to return straight home after school. It was her first day, after all.

Daisy was just about to enter the school yard when she saw the strangest sight. Surely that was Mr Wiggins climbing out of the classroom window! Daisy's mouth dropped open in astonishment. The next moment an arm appeared and a large brown sack was passed through the window.

Daisy, realising what was happening, took a sharp intake of breath. But what could she do about it? If she dashed across the yard towards Mrs Morris' room, Mr Wiggins would be sure to see her. She would never reach the school entrance. No, there was only one possible course of action. Daisy knew exactly what she had to do.

❋ ❋ ❋

Callum was hammering with his fists on the stockroom door. It was pitch black and he seemed to have been locked in for ages.

In truth, he had only been locked in for about fifteen minutes but Callum hated the dark. He always went to sleep with the light on. Callum was angry, too. He was angry that those two thugs and Mr Wiggins were getting away with the school laptops and there was nothing he could do about it. Callum hammered on the door again and screamed for help – but it was no good. He was all alone in the darkness and it was going to be a long, long night.

Callum sank back onto a pile of books and put his hands to his head in despair. Seconds later, he heard a familiar sound. It was a distinct click, just like the one he had heard as he was locked in the stockroom. The very next moment, the door opened and the small room was flooded with light.

To Callum's amazement, Daisy stepped forward, stared at him and said: 'Callum, what on earth are you doing in there?'

Callum could hardly believe she had asked such a stupid question. He took a deep breath and said: "Oh, I just thought I'd lock myself in for a joke!'

'Well I don't think that's very funny,' said Daisy, seriously. 'I was getting worried about you.'

'Come on out, lad,' said another deeper voice, and a tall man in a dark blue uniform stepped forward and reached out a helping hand towards Callum.

Once in the classroom, Callum was surprised to see several other people. As well as Daisy and the policeman, Mrs Morris was over by the window talking to the school caretaker. Callum was also aware of a blue

flashing light, which was coming from a police van parked outside the school gate.

'I don't understand,' said Callum, scratching his head, 'what's happened?'

'Don't you worry about a thing,' said the policeman. 'We've got those three thieves safely locked away in the van thanks to your sensible friend here.' He nodded towards Daisy, who flashed her eyelids and beamed with pleasure. 'She had the sense to ring the police on her mobile phone.'

'It's got a picture of Mr Tickle on it,' said Daisy, holding the phone up for Callum to see.

'We caught them red-handed thanks to this young lady,' continued the policeman. 'They didn't even get out of the school car park.'

'Well done, Daisy,' muttered Callum, reluctantly, 'and thanks for helping me.'

'No problem,' said Daisy, beaming with pleasure. 'I guess it was just your lucky day when you met me, wasn't it, Callum?'

Callum took a gulp and glanced up at the

blackboard. His eyes fixed on the date, which was printed boldly at the top of the board:

Friday the thirteenth!

Also available in the Reluctant Reader Series

Sam's Spitfire Summer *(WW2 Adventure)*
Ian MacDonald   ISBN 978 1 905637 43 0

Alien Teeth   *(Humorous Science Fiction)*
Ian MacDonald   ISBN 978 1 905637 32 2

Eyeball Soup   *(Science Fiction)*
Ian MacDonald   ISBN 978 1 904904 59 5

Chip McGraw   *(Cowboy Mystery)*
Ian MacDonald   ISBN 978 1 905637 08 9

Close Call   *(Mystery - Interest age 12+)*
Sandra Glover   ISBN 978 1 905 637 07 2

Beastly Things in the Barn   *(Humorous)*
Sandra Glover   ISBN 978 1 904904 96 0
www.sandraglover.co.uk

Cracking Up   *(Humorous)*
Sandra Glover   ISBN 978 1 904904 86 1

Deadline   *(Adventure)*
Sandra Glover   ISBN 978 1 904904 30 4

The Crash   *(Mystery)*
Sandra Glover   ISBN 978 1 905637 29 4

The Owlers   *(Adventure)*
Stephanie Baudet   ISBN 978 1 904904 87 8

The Curse of the Full Moon   *(Mystery)*
Stephanie Baudet   ISBN 978 1 904904 11 3

A Marrow Escape   *(Adventure)*
Stephanie Baudet   ISBN 1 900818 82 5

PUBLISHING

www.eprint.co.uk